ISBN: 9798432168351
Imprint: Independently published

visit www.ilariacapponiteixeira.myportfolio.com

To Orin, Sisu, Leo and Adam.

Thanks to MG, Ewa Jozefkowiczmy for their contribution,
to my sisters Marta and Reta for their help.
Thanks to my Family and Friends
for their trust and love.

Be myself

Written and illustrated by

ILARIA C. TEIXEIRA

Outside in the sun

Drew and Deedee

usually play

Where Deedee is already having fun

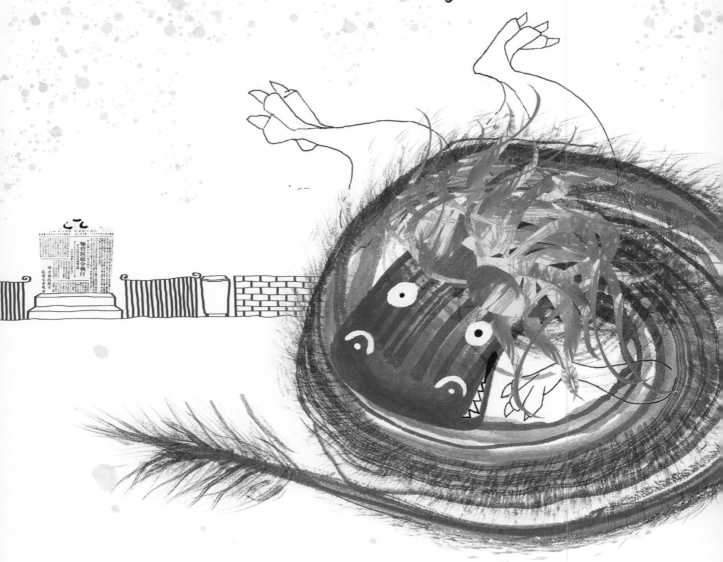

So fun!   So sweet!   Do it again!   How do you do that?

but Drew is still finding the way.

Sometimes it seems
that Deedee doesn't care,
that tail moves so fast

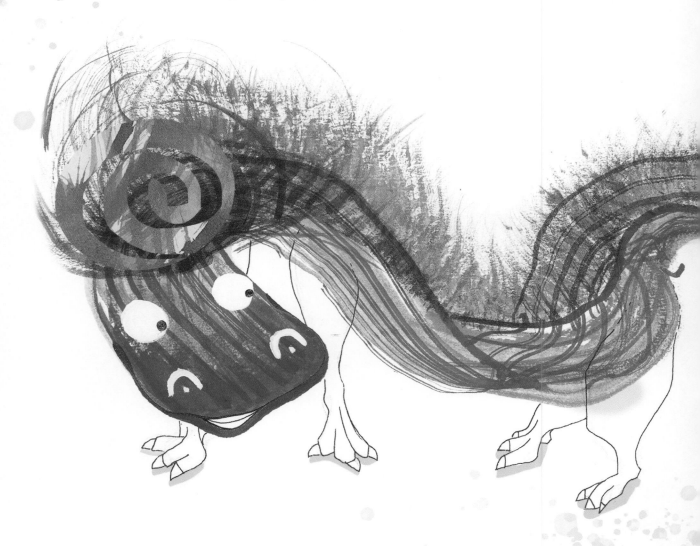

and Drew thinks "it's not fair!"

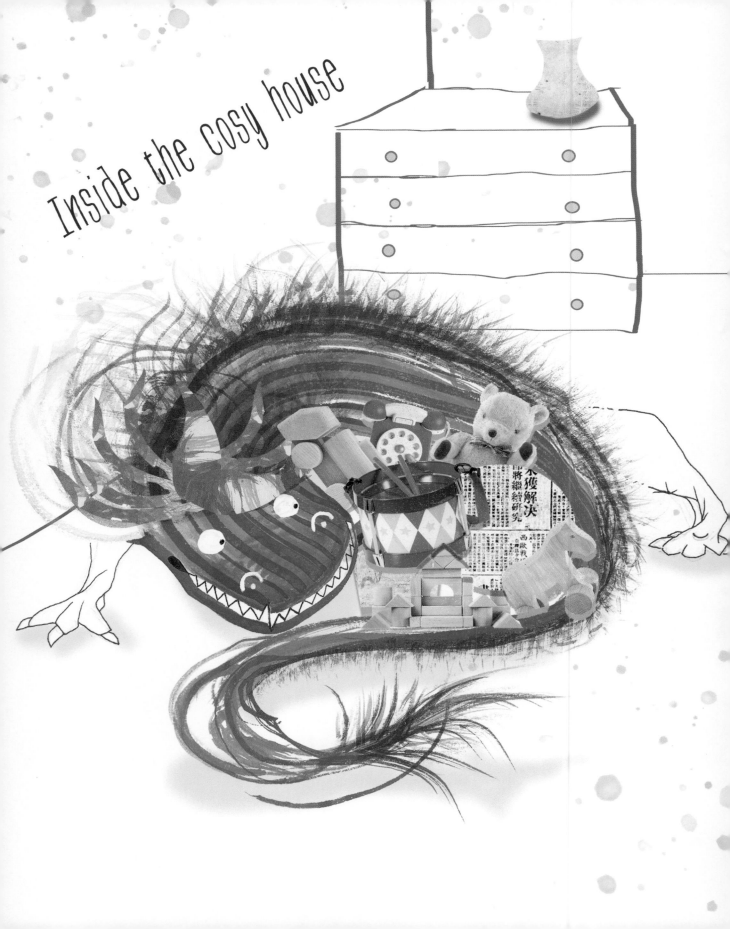

Inside the cosy house

Drew likes to take time to pick
the right toy

while Deedee is busy emptying
the toybox with excitment and joy

Drew feels a little lost
as Deedee

runs about the place...

But Deedee's puzzled
when Drew says
"JUST GIVE ME SOME SPACE!"

"Why does Deedee always act this way? Making a mess with the toys

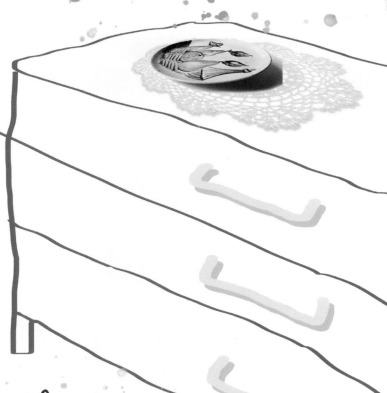

and runing so fast
when we play"

"Why does Drew always take so long to join in the fun

to pick the right toy and
gets upset when
I run?"

If only I could just do what I like

Ball say something,
help them please!

If only I could just do what I feel

With both of you

Even if you both

You are unique

and that's what I like,

because you

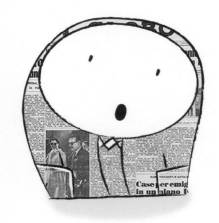

I do love to play

have a different way!

and wonderful

every day is different

are both right"

So smile at each other

you can play together or

And still be

because at the end

alone, be very different

the best of friends

And so from that day on, both with no fear,
Deedee and Drew put in some effort
to understand how to play together
and be more clear.

Do the things that you like in your unique way

just BE YOURSELF every single day

Remember that our differences

Make the whole world worth exploring

If we were all the same, well then ...

Life would be rather boring.

I love being MYSELF

Printed in Poland
by Amazon Fulfillment
Poland Sp. z o.o., Wrocław

89462399R00018